Tots and the
Curly-Tail Piglets

Written by Ragdoll

Illustrated by Penny Lane

A Ragdoll Production for Central Independent Television

Scholastic Children's Books,
Scholastic Publications Ltd,
7-9 Pratt Street, London NW1 0AE

Scholastic Inc.,
555 Broadway, New York, NY 10012-3999, USA

Scholastic Canada Ltd,
123 Newkirk Road, Richmond Hill,
Ontario, Canada L4C 3G5

Ashton Scholastic Pty Ltd,
PO Box 579, Gosford, New South Wales,
Australia

Ashton Scholastic Ltd,
Private Bag 92801, Penrose, Auckland,
New Zealand

Published by Scholastic Children's Books 1994
Text copyright © Ragdoll 1994
Illustrations copyright © Penny Lane 1994

Original script Robin Stevens, Anne Wood, Andrew Davenport.
Text adapted by Jack Ousbey

Design of Tots - TV puppets and house
copyright © Ragdoll Productions (UK) Ltd 1993
Central logo copyright © Central Independent Television plc 1989
Based on the Central Independent Television series produced by Ragdoll Productions

ISBN 0 590 55655 X

Typeset by Rapid Reprographics
Printed in Great Britain by Bath Press Colourbooks, Glasgow

All was quiet in the secret house where the Tots lived. Tilly woke up first.

"Bonjour, Tots," she said.

"Good morning, Tilly," said Tiny.

"Tots," said Tom, "I think something interesting is going to happen today. I have a feeling, I have."

Tiny took the magic bag from its peg and they were ready to go adventuring out.

"Eee-aw," said Donkey as they went through the garden.

"What will we see today?" sang the Tots. "What will we see?"

"Peek-a-boo," said Furryboo.

The Tots came out of the woods and into the big field where the farmer sometimes kept animals.

"Tom," said Tiny, "there's not a single thing to look at in this field."

"The farmer must have moved the animals somewhere else," said Tom.

"Qu'est-ce-que c'est?" Tilly asked, pointing.

"It looks like a little wooden house, without a roof," said Tiny.

"Tots," said Tom, "that's a pen, that is. And I think those snuffly noises we can hear are pigs."

7

The Tots peeped over the top of the wooden fence. Four piglets were snuffling and rooting for food in the grass. The smallest one was a black-spotted piglet.

"Regardez," said Tilly, "les grandes oreilles."

"Not only are they big ears," said Tiny, "they are pointy as well."

"Pointy, pointy ears," said Tom, "that's what they are."
The Tots laughed. They laughed even more when Tilly noticed what curly tails the piglets had, and how they snuffled as they searched for food. Then the Tots began to sing –

This little pig's got pointy,
pointy ears,
This little pig's got a curly,
whirly tail,
This little pig's got a
snuffly snout,
And this little pig goes...

Just then the little spotted pig found a hole at the bottom
of the fence and squeezed through into the field. Tiny ran
after it.

"Hey, you naughty little spotty piglet," he shouted.
"Come back."

He caught the runaway pig
and pushed him back into the pen.
Then he gathered up some straw
and stuffed it into the hole at the
bottom of the fence.

"That should keep you safe inside,
little pig," he said.

The Tots settled down to watch the piglets and once more they started their song –

This little pig's got a
snuffly snout,
This little pig's got pointy,
pointy ears,
This little pig's got a curly,
whirly tail,
And this little pig goes...

"Oh no," cried Tom, as the tiny piglet pushed away the straw bundle and squeezed out into the field again. "Oh, no, no, no, you naughty little runaway piglet!"

This time Tom recaptured the piglet. On his way back to
the pen, Tom picked a bunch of twigs from a bush in the
field. Once the piglet was safely back in the pen, he stuck
the ends of the twigs firmly into the ground, so that they
covered the hole in the fence.

Then Tom made up a little rhyme –

These little twiglets
Will keep these little piglets
Safely inside their pen.
Four little twiglets,
For four little piglets,
Now it's time for our song,
once again.

And Tiny, Tilly and Tom linked arms and began to sing –

This little pig's got a curly,
whirly tail,
This little pig's got a
snuffly snout,
This little pig's got pointy,
pointy ears,
And this little pig goes...

Then the naughty, black-spotted piglet knocked over the twigs and escaped for the third time.

"Alors," said Tilly. "Nous avons besoin du sac magique."

"You're right, we do need the magic bag," said Tiny. "We need it very urgently."

Tilly stood behind Tiny and spoke softly to the magic bag. "Sac magique," she said. "Sac magique."

Tiny could feel the magic bag jiggling and joggling on his back. He turned his head and saw something sticking up through the flap. It was made of wood. It was a small criss-cross shape. Tilly lifted it out and opened it up. It stretched out to make a little piece of fencing.

"Maintenant, mon petit cochon," said Tilly, bending down and picking up the spotted piglet. She put him back into the pen and then fixed the fencing in place.

The Tots set off back through the woods to the Secret House. As they walked, Tilly played the Going Back Home Song, and Tom and Tiny sang –

What a lovely morning,
Let's all give a shout,
We are coming home again,
We've been adventuring out.
We've seen a naughty piglet,
We've sung a piglet song.
Exploring done, here we come,
Back home where we belong.

"Tell you what, Tots," said Tom. "I have a good idea for a game, I have," and he whispered in their ears.

Inside the house, the Tots got out some glue, some card, some paint, some brushes and three pairs of scissors.

"There we are," sang Tom to himself as he cut and glued and painted. A bit more hair here. A bit more hair there, and we have a lovely card wolf. Mr Big Bad Wolf."

Tilly and Tiny were also making card masks on sticks. Their masks were pink pig faces, with snuffly noses.

"Hey Tots," shouted Tom. "Have you made the House of Pillows yet?"

"It's nearly ready," said Tiny. "Just wait until we get inside, Tom."

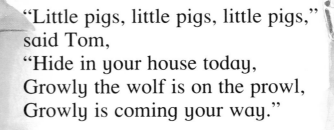

"Little pigs, little pigs, little pigs," said Tom,
"Hide in your house today,
Growly the wolf is on the prowl,
Growly is coming your way."

"Tom, excuse me," said Tiny. "Excuse me, Tom, but I would have quite liked to have been Mr Big Bad Wolf."

"Et moi, moi, moi," said Tilly.

"But I'm Mr Big Bad Wolf," said Tom. "And I like being him, I do."

"I think we should have turns at being the wolf, Tom," said Tiny.

"Oh, all right Tots," said Tom. "Let's play the game."

Tom crept up to the pillow-house with his big bad wolf
mask in front of him, making howly-growly noises. The
two little pigs watched from their window, getting more
and more anxious. The wolf huffed and puffed and blew,
and the pillow house shivered and shook.

Again he huffed and puffed,
so hard in fact, that the
pillow house collapsed around
the two little pigs. They
shouted and screamed and then
ran out into the garden
where there was an empty
blanket-house waiting for them.
Mr Big Bad Wolf followed.

"Excuse moi, Tom," said Tilly. "C'est mon tour maintenant."

"But I like being Mr Wolf, I do," said Tom.

"She's right, Tom," said Tiny. "It is her turn. Come and be a little pig with me, Tom."

"Eh, maintenant, je suis le loup," said Tilly in a very deep, howly-growly voice. "Et je vais souffler sur votre maison."

From inside their blanket house, Tom and Tiny saw Mr Big Bad Wolf creeping nearer and nearer. They watched as the wolf huffed and puffed and blew, harder and harder, until the blanket house wobbled and shook and then fell down on them.

"Run to the house of bricks," shouted Tom.

The Tots had made a brick house out of cardboard in the corner of the garden. Tilly the wolf followed them as they ran inside.

"Hang on a minute," said Tiny. "You have been Mr Big Bad Wolf for ages, Tilly. It's my turn now."

Tiny was Mr Wolf and Tilly joined Tom in the brick house.

"You know what this means, little pigs," growled Tiny. "I will have to huff, I will have to puff and I will have to blow your house down."

But when Tiny huffed, the house stayed firm. And when Tiny puffed, the house stayed firm. No matter how hard he blew he couldn't blow the house down.

"Tom, Tilly, I can't manage to blow this old brick house down," said Tiny, "and it's really part of the game, the blowing down bit. Tell you what, if I can't blow it down, can I knock it down?"

"Oui, d'accord," shouted Tilly.

"All right then, Tiny," said Tom.

Tiny ran to the other side of the garden. "Right, little pigs," he shouted. "I'm going to bump your house down. I'm going to thump your house down. And here I come!"

And Tiny ran so hard, he went right through the wall of
the house and ended up with Tom and Tilly, as the bricks
collapsed around them.

"C'etait super," said Tilly.

"What a great game," said Tiny.

"I thought you might like the Big Bad Wolf game,"
said Tom.

Later the Tots were tired. It was time for bed. As they went upstairs they heard Donkey "Eee-aw" goodnight from outside.

When they were curled up in their beds they sang – very softly – their Goodnight song.

We've had some adventures,
some songs and some fun,
It's time now for sleeping,
our busy day's done.
So it's Bonne Nuit, Tilly,
and Sleep Well, Tom.
It's Goodnight Tiny
– and everyone.

And very soon, all was quiet in the secret house where the Tots lived. And then from somewhere in the rafters, Furryboo gave a little "Peek-a-boo."